# Fatal Pursuit

*A Gripping Action-Adventure Political Thriller*

**Teagan Stone Series**
Book 8

# Ava S. King

304 Publishing Company

For questions and comments about this book, please contact 304 Publishing at info@304publishing.com. Visit the official website at www.authoravasking.com

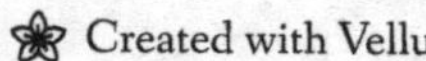 Created with Vellum

# Latest Releases: Ava S. King

Agent Red Fatal Memory: Teagan Stone Book 1

Agent Red Fatal Target: Teagan Stone Book 2

Agent Red Fatal Crime: Teagan Stone Book 3

Agent Red Fatal Justice: Teagan Stone Book 4

Agent Red Fatal Enemy: Teagan Stone Book 5

Mirror of Lies: Jessica Smith Book 1

Agent Red Fatal Death: Teagan Stone Book 6

Mirror of Lust: Jessica Smith Book 2

Agent Red Fatal Revenge: Teagan Stone Book 7

Agent Red Fatal Pursuit: Teagan Stone Book 8

Upcoming Releases (2024/2025)

Mirror of Danger: Jessica Smith Book 3

Chris Harris Mystery/Thriller Series

Agent Red Fatal Attack: Teagan Stone Book 9

Agent Red Fatal Mission: Teagan Stone Book 10

*I want to dedicate this book to my family and friends.*

*You are always with me, no matter where I go, and everything you've taught me has made me a better person.*

# Disclaimer

A work of fiction contains strong language and explicit content and is only intended for mature readers. The story may contain unconventional situations, language, and sexual encounters that may offend some readers. This book is for mature readers (18+).

# Introduction

Sign up for Ava S. King's mailing list for news, new releases, and special offers.

www.authoravasking.com

# Synopsis

**A fast-paced action adventure and political thriller with unforgettable characters and heart-pounding suspense.**

Teagan Stone is on foreign ground, once again trying to defend the country she has vowed to protect. US military weapons have been stolen, and Teagan has gone undercover to unravel a conspiracy before the weapons are used against them. In a race against time, Teagan identifies suspects but soon learns that danger lies much closer to home.

**Will Teagan unravel the plot against her country before their enemies prevail and war ensues?**

# Chapter One

Keeping a wary eye on the room, Morris waited with bated breath to see if anyone recognized him. A fine line of sweat prickled over his body as he counted the minutes until he succeeded in his mission and escaped without dying.

Keeping eye contact with the guards behind the world's most feared man, he gripped the envelope. Coming alone was stupid, but he had no choice if he was genuinely going to abandon his country. After placing the yellow envelope on the table, he slid it along the surface and sat down.

The room was quiet for five long seconds until his guest turned it over, opened it, and removed the photos.

Morris spoke in response to his guest's silence. "That's a sample of what I can bring," he spouted in a rush.

His guest raised his hand to stop him. "Where did you get these, and how do I know you're not lying?"

The stack of photos showed US government military-style weapons that only the highest clearance personnel should know about. Disclosing these to the prickly man in front of him put a target on Morris's back.

"My work is detailed and classified. I wouldn't come here unless I were sure I could give you proof."

The other man smiled at his words and placed the photos back in the envelope.

Morris relaxed in his seat, knowing his dreams were about to come true. But with the flick of his hand, the man opposite him proved that things could change in a split second.

Guns appeared at Morris's front and back, and he held his hands up in surrender. "What are you doing?" Nerves and fear caused sweat to drip from his brow.

Yashan Vasiliev, a renowned weapons dealer, stood to his full height of six feet three inches. At forty-two, with Yemen and Russian ancestry, he answered to no law or country unless money was the motivator. The empire he'd constructed during the past ten years caused fear and respect in his foes. When he'd received word of a man wanting to sell US military weapons, he set up this meeting to hear what he was trying to push. Caution was the primary goal. If he passed the test, he wouldn't need to kill him.

Morris's mouth was dry. He was scared out of his mind at what he'd gotten involved in because of his greed.

Yashan sat on the edge of the table and sneered at Morris. "Who knows you're here?"

Morris's stomach knotted. "Um, nobody. I promise."

Tapping his finger on the envelope, Yashan asked, "How did you get these pictures?"

Morris glanced at the envelope and back up at Yashan. "I stole them."

"Who do you work for?"

"I-I—" Panic jabbed at his stomach.

Yashan smirked at the spectacle in front of him. "Are you nervous, Morris?" He tilted his head. "It's interesting that you came here alone."

Morris's shoulder blades drew together. "I swear I never said a word to anyone."

"I don't believe you, Morris. These photos are too important for a little geek like you to have access."

"B-But you can't—"

He slumped in his chair with a bullet in his brain before he could finish his sentence.

"Clean up this mess and check out the car he arrived in," Yashan instructed.

Two of his guards lifted Morris's body from the chair and removed him from the room. Leonid, Yashan's right-hand man, approached him as the door closed and plucked the discarded envelope from the table.

"What?" Yashan waited for Leonid to speak.

"Are you sure that was necessary?"

Yashan shrugged and grinned.

Leonid chuckled. "If we secure these weapons, we'll make ten times what we made last year."

"China will be pleased."

"We only have a small amount of time to get those weapons."

"Yes, if the US becomes aware of the pictures." Yashan took the envelope from Leonid and headed for the awaiting car.

It was midnight in London, and he scanned the darkness as the rear door opened. He slid onto the back seat with Leonid on the other side.

Yashan dipped his hand into his pocket and removed

a bag of peanuts. He tossed some into his mouth, staring out the window at Big Ben as their driver pulled away. His phone buzzed, and he pulled it out to see a text.

"If an opportunity presents itself, we have to take it if the money is high." Leonid pressed.

**Unknown:** *Any response?*

**Yashan:** *Made contact.*

Arriving at the rented house, Yashan exited the car and headed inside as Leonid was driven away. He closed the door behind him and dropped the keys on the hallway table. In the office, he logged into his computer and removed the pictures from the envelope. Yashan smirked at the US government database after verifying the identification of each photo. Hacking into a country's military intelligence gave him a high second only to killing someone.

Yashan smirked. "Клеаранче."

* * *

Teagan's phone cut through her sleep.

Christian forced one eye open and checked the time on the nightstand. "It's two a.m.," he groaned, climbing out of bed and heading for the bathroom.

Teagan opened her eyes and sat up slowly, grabbing her phone. "Mr. President."

"Agent Stone, we have a problem."

Teagan checked the time again. "Sir?"

"I know you're on vacation in the UK."

Teagan heard the toilet flush and the faucet turn off before Christian trekked back to the bed and tossed the comforter over his head. They'd spent the day running around with the kids, enjoying time away.

"I am, Sir."

"Check your email," President Sanders instructed.

Teagan crawled out of bed wearing Christian's pajama pants and a large t-shirt. Removing her laptop from her briefcase, she sat in the corner of her suite and turned it on. She scrolled to her Gmail account to see a high-level alert from an unverified account.

"*Weapons chemist and state employee Morris Rogers missing.*" Teagan read the description.

"Cancel your vacation. I need you on a call," the president stated.

Teagan's shoulders sagged. "Sir, do you know what time it is?"

"Too late for anyone to go back to sleep," President Sanders replied before ending the call.

Staring at the phone, Teagan stared at her laptop, feeling defeated.

"We're not canceling our trip," Christian grumbled.

Placing the computer on the couch, Teagan headed to the bathroom. Ten minutes later, she was dressed. She grabbed her phone, purse, and laptop and bent to kiss Christian's cheek. "We're not canceling the trip. I need to step out for a minute, and then I can catch up with you and the kids."

Popping one eye open, Christian nodded. He grabbed her hand and squeezed. "I think the boys want to go sightseeing."

"Make sure Tatum doesn't go shopping without me." Teagan stood with her arm outstretched.

Christian tightened his hold. "Be careful."

Smiling, Teagan kissed his palm and left the room. She halted at the stairs in front of two men wearing suits.

One of the guards held the door open. "Director Stone?"

"Yes."

"We have your car waiting, ma'am." The guards led her to the waiting car.

Teagan scrubbed a hand over her face. "Where are we going?"

"To the US embassy, ma'am," the other guard replied.

"No, that's too obvious."

The guards glanced at each other.

"Excuse me, ma'am?" the first guard asked.

"Take me to the MI5 offices."

The guard took a faltering step. "The MI5 offices?"

"The story you're about to hear is confidential."

"Director Stone, we have orders to bring you to the US Embassy."

"Understood, but your orders have changed. I promise you won't get fired."

Both their cell phones rang. The first guard answered, and she waited for confirmation. He ended the call and gave the driver new directions. "Take Director Stone to the MI5 building."

Jude Fessonhay, her counterpart, greeted Teagan when they arrived a short time later. "Sorry to wake you so early."

"Am I the only one they could call, Jude?" Teagan asked with a raised eyebrow.

Shoving the door open, Jude motioned for her to take a seat. Teagan wanted to be back in bed with her husband, waiting for her kids to come in and wake them up for breakfast. Slouching into a seat, Teagan waited for Jude to speak.

"I have your team on a video call, along with the president." Jude pressed a switch, activating the connection.

Spider, Broderick, Daughtry, and Gregory appeared on one screen, and President Sanders on another. Teagan leaned forward and nodded at the men as Jude moved to the corner and crossed his arms over his chest.

"Morris Rogers worked for the Department of Defense and State," Jude said as a picture of Morris came on the screen.

"Rogers is a specialist in weapons chemistry. He's missing," President Sanders informed the group.

"What the hell?" Daughtry muttered.

Clearing her throat, Teagan asked, "Anything special we need to be aware of, Mr. President?"

President Sanders stroked his beard. "Yashan Vasiliev was spotted in town."

"Oh, shit." Daughtry choked on his drink.

"Jude." Teagan waved him over.

"Yes, Director Stone?" Jude approached her.

She stabbed a finger at Daughtry on the screen. "Mute him."

Jude pressed the mute button on Daughtry.

Teagan turned her attention back to the president. "Mr. President, what are you asking of us?"

# Chapter Two

*We believe Morris Rogers has stolen US weapons.*

Teagan recalled the comment as she sat in the back of the car in London on Saturday morning. The president sanctioned her search with her team to keep the details out of the media. In addition, Yashan Vasiliev's presence in the country raised a red flag for the president.

Dropping her bag on the floor, Teagan strode into the hotel suite with a big smile, clutching the donut box and hot chocolate. The kids were on the floor watching TV and laughing.

"Mommy!" Cole jumped up and ran to take the box of donuts from her hand.

Teagan sat on the couch with her hot chocolate and tucked her feet beneath her. "What are we watching?" she asked as CJ and Tatum picked out their favorite donuts.

Tatum crawled up next to her, laying her head in her

lap. "Peppa Pig." She took Teagan's phone from her pocket to play games.

"Where's your dad?"

"Right here." Christian entered the room holding a brochure and a pair of shoes and sat beside Teagan.

"Going somewhere?"

He grabbed a chocolate donut. "We have the tour of Buckingham Palace, remember?"

"Yeah, Mom. We'll do some shopping after that." Tatum kicked her legs in the air in excitement.

"Let me shower and get some food in my stomach." Teagan leaned over to kiss Christian, and the kids grimaced at the PDA.

Trailing after her, Christian described what he planned for today's sightseeing. Teagan picked an outfit from the closet while Christian sat on the bed. He nodded at her choice as she held up wide-leg pants and a baggy t-shirt with *I love London* on it.

"Will the President need you during our entire vacation?"

Teagan grabbed her shower cap from the suitcase. "I don't know, babe."

She quickly showered and dried off, twisting her hair into a high ponytail. Christian was waiting on the bed when she emerged from the bathroom, so she crawled beside him.

"It would make sense if the president looked for someone to take over the firm." Christian rubbed her scalp, pulling her close.

"I like my job."

"Seriously, he needs to figure out a way not to call you at all hours of the night."

Teagan sighed. "We need to get going."

Christian waited while Teagan dressed and slid on her heels. Locking hands, they headed to the living room. Teagan picked up her purse, and the kids trailed their parents outside just as her phone rang.

"Hello."

"The president wants an answer by Monday morning," Gregory said, wasting no time.

Teagan paused on the curb. "I need everyone on a flight here soon as possible."

"Teagan!" Christian called.

Teagan gestured for him to give her a minute. "Have Spider call the US Embassy and tell them we need a log of all employees."

"How's London?" Gregory asked.

"We've spent one day here, and the kids are ready to spend our last dime."

Gregory chuckled and promised to see her soon before ending the call.

Teagan put on her shades and hopped into the family van, where Jason, their driver, was waiting to take them to their destination. Two undercover security cars wove into the traffic, one in front and one behind. She talked with Tatum about where she wanted to shop while the boys played on their Gameboys.

Tatum leaned over her mother to look out the window. "Where are we going first?"

"Buckingham Palace."

"Can we meet the Queen?" Cole asked, looking up from his game.

"The Queen passed away. They have a King now," Teagan explained.

Watching the crowds gather near the front, Teagan

took in the scene, holding Tatum's hand as she waited for the car to stop. Jason came around to help them, and Christian grabbed Cole's hand as the family gathered.

"We're here. Make sure you stay close," Teagan said.

"Dad, I want to be like him." Cole pointed at the changing of the guard.

"You want to live in London?" Christian teased, pulling on his hat.

"I can't do it back home?" Cole's face screwed in annoyance.

Christian exclaimed, "No, only here, buddy."

Removing her phone, Teagan nudged the kids to stand together. "Tatum, stand next to your brothers so I can get a picture."

"See how big the place is?" Christian remarked.

"I want to live here," Tatum pleaded.

Teagan watched the kids have fun with their dad. An hour into sightseeing, they decided to get something to eat. Tatum sat beside her mom with her two shopping bags at the restaurant near the palace.

Christian ordered their food while Teagan handed them all a glass of water.

"Smile wide, Tatum." Teagan directed, pulling out her phone to take pictures.

She laughed at Tatum as she posed. Her grin widened as she watched her boys go back and forth on the taste of the food. She loved these moments when everything was simple and filled with joy.

"Mommy, did you take the picture?" Tatum asked, touching her hand.

Teagan yanked her attention back to Tatum. "One more. Smile big."

Their server appeared with food of different varieties to try.

"Babe, you want some of the sandwiches?" Christian offered.

"A little. Cole, please wipe your mouth." Teagan giggled at the milk mustache on his upper lip. London was a week-long trip while the kids were on spring break. After returning from Jamaica seven months ago, they'd planned a couples getaway, as well as of London.

* * *

Christian came out of the kids' bedroom later that evening as Teagan slipped into her jacket and shoes. He walked up behind her as she grabbed her briefcase, circling her waist and kissing her shoulder. "How long should I stay up?"

She placed her hand over his. "Don't. Tonight's going to be long."

The press would have a field day if they knew a special agency from the US was in the country working to take down a criminal.

Christian stroked his fingers through her hair. "I'm always sharing you with the president."

"There's only one person I love, and that's you." She stepped out of his embrace and turned to kiss him.

He smiled. "Good. Be safe, and call me when you can."

"I will." Teagan strolled through the suite and opened the door to four guards. She glanced back at her husband as she left, and they shared a smile.

Once in the car, Teagan took her phone out to scroll

through her email. The man who looked like Yashan replayed in her mind. Nothing popped up from her team as she checked her mail. It was early morning, and she'd hoped they would arrive by the time she got to the US embassy.

Security allowed them to pull in and park outside. Climbing out of the car, Teagan walked behind her guards into the building and through the lobby. The loud voices and phone calls were muted as she entered the office of the US ambassador.

"Teagan, thank you for coming." Secretary of State Shaw Linden stood up to greet her, along with Ambassador Asher.

"Mr. Secretary. I had no idea you were here." Teagan offered her hand.

Shaw reached out to shake it. "Please, sit. I informed Ambassador Henley at the last minute after talking with the president."

Teagan sat in the chair. Secretary Shaw and Ambassador Asher fixed their eyes on each other before speaking.

"I feel like you're about to drop a bomb on me." Teagan laid the briefcase on her lap.

"Your team is on the way, but we wanted to inform you ahead of time," Ambassador Asher said.

"What?" Teagan looked from Asher to Shaw.

"This is a sensitive issue. We tried to capture someone in Interpol a few years ago," Shaw said.

Teagan sat up at his declaration. "Who?"

Shaw gave her a file. "A weapons dealer named Yashan Vasiliev."

"He's a dangerous man, Teagan, and he's in London."

Asher pulled up his photo. "The president sent you here to capture or kill him."

Teagan flipped open his file, scanning what they'd discovered so far. Yashan had been slipping in and out of different countries selling weapons to anyone who could meet his fee.

# Chapter Three

**T**wo Days Later

Daughtry rested his head on the table. He'd woken up alone in his hotel room with a hangover from drinking the night before. He'd slipped up. Wanting to relax for once before he delved deeper into the mission, he met a woman in a bar and took her back to his room. He didn't expect to wake up alone with her things gone, along with his phone. The first person he notified was Gregory to check the security cameras, but the woman had dodged them, and they didn't have a close-up of her face. Sadly, Daughtry couldn't remember her features clearly either due to excess alcohol.

"Run it back again, Daughtry." Teagan slammed her hand on the table.

Shaw and Asher were waiting for an update on Yashan's whereabouts. In the meantime, Teagan's family were waiting to spend time together before they left.

Daughtry ran his hands over his face. "I went to a club with a few friends."

"Friends who live here in London, and without your guards, correct?" Teagan growled.

"Listen, Teagan—"

"Explain the facts. No excuses, Daughtry," Teagan cut him off.

Daughtry leaned back in his chair. "All I remember is that we talked at the bar and went back to my hotel room."

Teagan and Spider made eye contact.

"No trace of her in the hotel video, Gregory?" Teagan asked.

Gregory hesitated, looking at the video from the bar on the big screen. "I got a copy of the footage from the bar. She stays low on camera."

"Daughtry, you're one of our top agents, and you didn't notice she was behaving suspiciously?" Teagan questioned.

"Teagan, we're not all married with families. I needed to let off some steam," Daughtry argued.

Teagan glowered. "There's letting off steam, and then there's waking up with a hangover and classified government information in the hands of the enemy."

Spider stood to ease the tension. Teagan was right. Daughtry knew it too, but his pride wouldn't let him admit he'd fucked up. "Teagan, we can handle Daughtry later. Have you heard from the President?"

"Yashan Vasiliev is here, along with the Secretary of State," Teagan replied.

"I haven't heard that name in over five years," Gregory commented.

"Same," Broderick agreed.

"Do you think Yashan had something to do with Morris Rogers' disappearance?" Spider wondered.

"More than likely. Morris was trying to sell US military weapons across the pond." Teagan gave them copies of her notes from her meeting with Shaw and Asher.

Broderick frowned. "What evidence do they have besides a theory?"

Teagan's frustration increased. All she'd wanted was a peaceful vacation, and her team had become increasingly strained over the past few months. Broderick was handling more tasks on his own in the private sector. Spider was holding meetings to delegate duties so Teagan could be home more. Daughtry and Gregory were coming in later and later after partying like college kids.

"Teagan, I apologize for not being on top of things as usual." Daughtry consumed more water to clear his headache.

"The president needs us to handle Morris's disappearance and Yashan's presence in London," Teagan explained.

"I gave a description of the woman to Gregory as best I could remember, and we canvased the hotel to see if anyone remembers her," Daughtry announced.

"Handle it before I have to." Teagan stood and left the conference room.

Spider jumped up to follow her. Teagan stomped into the temporary office the Embassy had provided. She slammed the door and tossed her purse on the couch, pacing back and forth.

Spider waited for her to calm down. "Relaxed now?"

Teagan waved him off. "He got wasted and left with a woman who stole his phone."

"Daughtry knows he messed up." Spider cracked his knuckles.

Teagan threw her hands on her hips. "I could wring his neck."

Spider surveyed her thoughtfully. "Can I be honest?"

"You're always honest."

"Foul play," Spider said.

She blinked at him. "What?"

"It's interesting that Daughtry wakes up missing his phone at the same time Morris goes missing."

Teagan stopped pacing and turned to face him. "That *is* coincidental."

Spider nodded. "It's perfectly played. We get called here, and Daughtry becomes a target."

"How did they know he'd be at the bar?" Teagan questioned.

"Probably followed him. Same way we follow targets."

"Shit." Teagan plopped down on the couch.

"Are the kids enjoying London?" Spider sat on the couch next to her.

"Yeah. They're supposed to fly back today."

"Let me look into Morris a little more. Gregory can handle the woman from the bar."

Teagan's throat tightened. "What should I do?"

"Spend time with your family."

She raised an eyebrow. "Are you after my job?"

"Hell, no." Spider chuckled as he stood. "Never was the type to handle stuffy suits like the secretary of state and ambassador."

Teagan gathered her purse and rose the couch. "I'm meeting with Jude to see if he has any news on Morris and Yashan."

"You need me to come with you?"

"No, I can handle it on my own. Get me some updates on Daughtry's missing woman." Before Teagan could grab her jacket, the desk phone rang. "Director Stone," Teagan answered, perching on the edge of the desk.

"I have Secretary of State Shaw Linden, ma'am," the operator said.

"Thank you."

"Teagan, I spoke with the president, and naturally, we have some early rumblings." The alarm in Shaw's voice suggested they prepare for the worst.

Spider stood over her desk as she placed the call on speaker.

Shaw spoke to someone in the background before resuming the call. "Sorry. I needed to get an update before we talked."

"Sir, I have you on speaker with my colleague."

"This is Spider, Mr. Secretary."

"After going through surveillance footage, we know Morris was selling weapons to foreign enemies. We know what it could mean if the US has to go to war again," Shaw said heavily.

"The footage should be sent to my team immediately, Mr. Secretary."

"Already on the way, Director Stone."

"Anything else, Sir?"

Shaw sighed. "Yashan was spotted at a bar in London."

"Name of the bar?" Spider reached into his pocket for his phone.

"The Night Jar," Shaw answered.

Teagan waited for Spider to confirm.

"Sir, can I call you back?" Teagan asked.

"I have back-to-back calls with the president and other leaders. Is there something I should know?"

"As of right now, we have nothing." Teagan gestured for Spider not to speak to avoid Daughtry being pulled into an interrogation situation.

"Keep me informed, Director Stone. While President Sanders is familiar with your style, I am not," Shaw stated.

* * *

Daughtry retraced his steps in the hotel room with Gregory and Broderick. Replacing his phone wasn't the problem. His job was on the line, and he needed to find the woman. Daughtry had worked for the agency for years without a blemish on his reputation, and the one time he'd relaxed his defenses, it had all gone horribly wrong.

Gregory searched through the closet while Broderick handled the bathroom. Daughtry remembered entering the room and pouring a drink for her and him.

"How long did it take before you two ended up in bed after you left the bar?" Gregory asked.

"Not long. Maybe ten or fifteen minutes." Daughtry lifted the glasses to bag up for fingerprints.

"Teagan will be pissed if we come back with nothing." Gregory emerged from the closet.

Daughtry huffed. "No one's more pissed than me. Bitch stole my phone."

"Did you have a lot of information stored on there?" Gregory shoved the blinds back to look out the window.

The hotel room was on the fifth floor, so she couldn't have jumped.

"I found something." Broderick stomped out of the bathroom, holding a napkin.

Daughtry frowned. "A napkin?"

"Lipstick," Broderick grunted, bagging it with the other evidence.

"Housekeeping hasn't cleaned up yet," Gregory mumbled.

"I told them it was a police situation and to block it off," Daughtry explained.

"We need to get the lipstick traced as soon as possible," Broderick said.

Daughtry nodded as they left the room and headed back to the car. "Faster we find her, the better."

President Sanders had sent Shaw in his place, but they all knew it was a matter of time before he showed up because one of them had screwed up an important mission.

Closing the car door, Daughtry leaned his head against the seat and closed his eyes, trying to recall her features. All the men at the bar had wanted to talk to her, and it hadn't surprised him when she approached him. Looking back, he'd been a pawn all along. She'd offered him drinks and flirted with him.

Daughtry's eyes popped open. "Go to The Night Jar."

"Why?" Gregory asked.

"I want to talk to the bartender." Daughtry excelled in his training. What he hated more than anything was a liar, and if the staff had been in on the woman's plan, each and every one of them would have hell to pay.

# Chapter Four

Yashan had never been impressed by anything or anyone in all his years of business. Having no allegiance to any country made him unpredictable, leaving leaders worldwide hesitant to get involved.

Mei Jing had come into his realm courtesy of President Jun Zang of China. Yashan met Mei Jing on his first visit to China and recognized that she was similar to him—she had loyalty to no one. Mei was an adviser and spy, traveling the world under the pretense of wanting to build foreign relations for her country. Deep down, she hated what happened to her family during the Taiwan and China conflict. As a trained soldier, she'd worked toward revenge for years.

When Yashan acquired information from Morris on military weapons, she'd fished for details on when Yashan would be setting up the sale and headed to London. Mei believed she could force a war between Russia and the US, but China would come out on top. The satisfaction of seeing her enemies crumble gave her the ultimate pleasure.

Taking the champagne glass from the tray, Mei lifted it to her lips and gestured at Yashan through the crowd before sauntering over to him. Political leaders talked and laughed as the party continued following Jun Zang's speech earlier that night.

"I hope we have a mutual understanding," Mei murmured to Yashan, smiling politely at the older couple walking past.

"Morris is no longer a problem."

"I have something for you." Mei opened her purse and removed a cell phone.

Yashan's eyebrow hiked upward.

"A little night out brought fruitful results. If you plan on selling the information to my boss, I want a bigger cut," Mei emphasized.

"The deal was seventy-thirty." Yashan reached out for the phone.

Mei yanked it back. "Deals change."

Yashan smirked and leaned forward to whisper, "Remind yourself, little one."

"You want what I have."

"Nothing comes at a price unless I say so."

"Morris Rogers?"

"A complication that will not come up again."

"Says the last man to see him alive."

"Are you trying to piss me off, Mei?"

Mei gulped the rest of her champagne as Jun Zang laughed loudly with his guests. The door opened to a beautiful woman with golden brown skin, high cheekbones, and long red hair parted down the middle.

"Who is that woman?" Mei pointed in her direction.

Yashan looked toward the entrance of the ballroom. He'd never seen a woman that sexy in his life. Striking deep-set cat eyes, pouty lips, and smooth curves in a black long-sleeved dress. "Must be someone important to come to the President's dinner."

"Maybe I should introduce myself." Mei finished her drink and headed for the woman.

Yashan grabbed her elbow and pulled her back. "Remember what I said."

Mei jerked out of his hold. "Fifty-Fifty."

Yashan released her. He hated having to kill, but he wouldn't tolerate Mei stepping on his toes and trying to extort more money from him. He stood in the corner as Mei introduced herself to the new guest. He wanted a taste of the redhead.

Mei stepped forward, reaching out a hand to Teagan. "Hello. I believe I would have remembered a face like yours on the President's guest list."

Teagan smiled at the compliment. She straightened her necklace for a better visual for Gregory to capture. Sliding her hair over her shoulder, she grasped Mei's hand. "Evie Nithercott," she said in her best English accent.

"Who do you work for, Evie?" Mei questioned.

"No one."

Mei seemed suspicious of her answer.

Teagan chuckled, grabbing a glass of champagne as a waiter passed by. "Can you keep a secret?"

Mei winked. "Please. I work for the president of China."

Teagan leaned closer, holding onto her necklace and aiming it to grab screenshots of the other guests. "My job is top secret, but I feel like I can trust you...?" Teagan let her words trail off in a question.

"Mei Jing. Advisor to President Zang," Mei supplied.

"Nice to meet you, Mei Jing. I'm former MI5."

Mei glowered, rooted to the spot at her statement. "How did you get an invite?"

"Well, if I tell you, I'd have to kill you." Teagan laughed as President Zang approached them.

"Mei, introduce me to your friend," President Zang said.

"Your Excellency, this is Evie Nithercott. I'm not sure she's a friend yet." Mei chortled. Teagan smiled, greeting President Zang. "It's an honor to meet you, President Zang."

The hostess of the evening encouraged everyone to take their seats. The entire evening was a celebration of the president of China and the prime minister of the UK coming together for peaceful talks. The US and the UK were long-time partners, and China could be a controlling factor in the Russian disputes.

"Evie, you say you're former MI5. Aren't you a secret spy?" Mei joked, taking a seat across from her.

"In a former life, protecting my country. As you would do for your country."

After finalizing a plan to discover what had happened to Morris, Teagan went undercover as her family flew back to the US. She'd promised to call her husband and kids soon. Then she transformed into Agent Red for the evening. Broderick and Spider slipped in as waitstaff, following the motto of never going anyplace without backup. Teagan came alone, hoping that her guise as a disgruntled former MI5 agent would entice the terrorists to spill their secrets.

The entire room fell quiet as a traditional *guqin* was played. Teagan sat back, looking at each face as President Zang and the UK Prime Minister whispered to each other. Her gaze landed on the one person she wasn't expecting to see tonight.

Teagan dipped her head at the man, and he raised his drink slightly in return. The food arrived and was placed in front of each guest. After the meal, the music paused as the prime minister gave a speech.

An hour later, Teagan picked up her purse and rose from her seat, heading for the bathroom. Glancing over her shoulder, she saw Mei eye them angrily as Yashan left his seat to follow her. Teagan pressed her earring to ensure the recording device was ready.

"Heading to the bathroom," she whispered.

"Loud and clear," Gregory replied.

Teagan sauntered down the hallway, passing Spider holding a tray of drinks,

"Ma'am, would you like more champagne?" he asked politely.

"No, thank you." Teagan raised her finger to motion behind herself at Yashan coming down the hallway.

Spider smiled at him. "Sir, would you like more champagne?"

Yashan ignored him and continued walking.

Teagan entered the bathroom and placed her purse on the counter, releasing a breath. She glanced at herself in the mirror before closing her eyes and saying a prayer.

"Evie Nithercott. You are Evie Nithercott," she repeated to herself.

Smoothing her hair, she checked over her makeup. She was ready to confront Yashan and get home to her family. Straightening her spine, she became Agent Red with a stoic face and no morals. Swiping her purse off the counter, she opened the door. She promptly dropped it, startled by Yashan standing in the hallway, blocking her from leaving.

"Excuse me," Teagan said, bending to retrieve it.

Yashan grabbed it first, causing their hands to touch. "A beautiful woman should never have to stoop to pick up an object," Yashan said in a flirty tone.

Teagan eyed him, wetting her lips. "What should she do?"

Yashan stepped closer so his chest brushed hers. "The only reason I would have you on your knees is to pleasure me."

Teagan raised an eyebrow and planted a hand on her hip. "Can I have your name before I pleasure you, sir?"

Yashan grinned. "Yashan Vasiliev."

"Evie Nithercott."

"If you didn't come alone, I suggest you leave and tell your date his time is up."

"Bold, Mr. Vasiliev."

He held her gaze as he ran a finger over her necklace. "Something tells me you like a bold man."

Teagan stuck her hand out. "I do, but can I have my purse back?"

He slowly laid the purse in her hand before tucking a strand of hair behind her ear. "Why don't we get out of here."

"And do what?"

"I can think of a lot of things."

"Lead the way," Teagan replied.

Yashan lifted her hand to kiss her knuckles and led her from the party.

Mei Jing watched with a scowl and followed them to

the limo reserved for Yashan. Daughtry was outside in the parked van and noticed Mei standing at the top of the steps. He wanted to jump out and snatch her up. Gregory stopped him as the limo with Teagan and Yashan drove off.

"Chill. We can't do anything right now," Gregory stated.

"That's her," Daughtry barked, scanning the area.

Mei turned to head back inside and bumped into Spider.

"Idiot!" she yelled as food spilled on her gown.

"I apologize, ma'am," Spider said.

"I'll have you fired for incompetence," Mei snapped as more staff came running at the commotion.

Needing to get away, Spider motioned to Broderick to slip out. They moved to the front door as Mei screamed for them to be fired. They jumped into the waiting van, and Gregory took off after the limo, following the tracking device in Teagan's necklace.

# Chapter Five

Yashan ran his hand up Teagan's thigh as she sat in the back seat resisting the temptation to put a bullet in his head. Her anxiety from working undercover with Diego came back to her when she had to pretend to have feelings for a man to save her country.

"What do you do, Mr. Vasiliev?"

"A bit of everything." Yashan took out his phone to reply to a text message.

"Are you married?"

He smiled, watching her for any hint of lying. "Does that matter?"

"No."

"Good."

Teagan crossed one leg over the other, revealing more of her thigh. Inside, she was Teagan praying to get through the night and make it out safely.

"Mr. Vasiliev, do you want to sleep with me?"

"Yashan."

"Yashan, do you want to sleep with me?"

"I do."

"Good. Then you won't mind giving me something in return."

"What is it you want in return, Ms. Nithercott?"

"Evie," Teagan corrected.

"Evie."

"I know who you are and what you do."

Yashan froze at her comment, dragging his eyes from Teagan to his driver. He removed a pack of cigarettes and a lighter from his pocket, extending one to Teagan. She took one and leaned in so he could light it.

"What is it you think I do, Evie?"

"Let's just say we're in the same line of business."

Yashan chuckled. "Are we now?"

"Yes. The business of making money," Teagan pressed, reading his body language.

Yashan pulled on his cigarette and placed his hand back on her thigh. "Money is my favorite thing next to sex."

Teagan placed her hand on his and moved it further up her thigh to her hip.

Wrapping his hand around her neck, he pulled her in until their lips were close but not touching. "Who do you work for?"

Teagan smiled and exhaled smoke in his face, giving no indication of the fear churning in her stomach. "Myself."

The limo pulled up outside a house twenty minutes from the city. Teagan wished it wasn't so secluded. Darkness surrounded them as most of the streetlights were out, and the nearest house was a few blocks away.

Yashan released her. "Get out."

He climbed out of the limo, tossing his cigarette to the

ground. He rounded the vehicle to the front steps of the property.

"Are we going to talk business or pleasure, Yashan?" Teagan crossed her arms over her chest.

"Depends on what pleasure I receive."

"Touché." Teagan tried to stall to ensure Gregory and the team made it here in time.

Teagan trailed behind Yashan as he ascended the steps and unlocked the door. She followed him into a cozy home with pictures of a family of four on the wall.

"Is this your family?"

"No."

Teagan paused, not wanting to move further inside. "Who lives here?"

"You ask a lot of questions, Evie."

"I like to ensure I won't lose money before I do business with anyone."

"The picture is a former business associate."

"Former?"

"He died."

"How?"

"Owed me money." Yashan shrugged, stepping further into the living room. Leaving the lights off, he grabbed a bottle of bourbon from the bar.

"You killed him?"

"Come take a seat on the couch so we can talk."

"Answer my question first."

He gulped the drink and poured another one. "Take your clothes off."

"First, business."

"I like you... feisty American."

"My father was American, and my mother was British," Teagan lied.

Yashan moved to sit on the couch, drinking the rest of his bourbon. He trailed his eyes from the top of Teagan's head to her feet, admiring her sexy silhouette and breasts.

"Weapons are only for sale for the right amount."

"Which amount is that?"

"Twenty million."

"When can I see them?"

Laughing, Yashan stood and went back to the bar. "Show me the money first."

"Do I look like a liar to you, Yashan?"

"Anyone can lie."

"True. I'll have the money ready to transfer when I've seen the product."

"Nothing will be seen until I get my money."

"What do I have to do—"

A loud knock at the door cut Teagan off, and Yashan's driver burst through the door. "Sir!"

"I told you not to disturb me," Yashan hissed, slamming his glass on the table.

Bowing his head in respect, the guard nervously walked further into the room and whispered in Yashan's ear. Yashan stalked to the front door. "You have to go."

"What about our deal?" Teagan followed him as his guard locked the door.

"Give me twenty million, and we can talk."

"Military grade weapons."

Yashan yanked open the door of the waiting limo, slid in, and rolled the window down. "Something worth purchasing."

The driver jumped into the front seat and started the vehicle. Teagan waited until the taillights of the limo faded before grabbing something from her purse and heading back up the steps to the house. A van pulled up, and her team jumped out, running up the steps as Teagan unlocked the door using the tech device that Gregory built for missions.

"How much did you get?" she asked, removing her heels and replacing them with the pair of flats Gregory passed her.

Gregory dropped her heels into a bag. "Everything from you entering the party to Yashan leaving a few minutes ago."

The team split up and searched the house while Teagan opened and closed drawers, trying to find clues to the family living there.

Teagan emphasized. "He ran out of here so fast that I didn't get a chance to slip a tracker on him."

"The woman you talked to was the girl who stole my phone," Daughtry said, coming out of the kitchen empty-handed.

Broderick held up a flashlight in the living room, shoving cushions to the side. Gregory went upstairs to help Spider search the bedrooms.

"Mei Jing."

"Who?" Daughtry's nose scrunched in confusion.

"The woman you pointed out is Mei Jing, advisor to the president of China."

Daughtry froze at her announcement. "Fucking spy."

"She played you and probably a lot of other men." Teagan left the dresser drawer and headed down the hall to the empty bathroom.

Daughtry yelled, "Fuck!"

Teagan opened and closed the cabinets, but nothing

seemed out of place. Deep in thought, she planted her hands on her hips as she considered their next move.

"Nothing up here," Spider said as he and Gregory came back downstairs.

Teagan sighed. "This is not good. We have a call with the president tomorrow, and we've got nothing."

"Maybe he'll come back tonight, and we can grab him," Daughtry suggested.

"That would only work if he lived here. I doubt Yashan would backtrack. He's used to moving around." Teagan looked out the window at the empty street.

They left the house and piled inside the van. Gregory started the engine, driving in the opposite direction to Yashan earlier.

No one noticed the female in the car trailing them. Mei Jing wondered what their connection was to Yashan.

* * *

A week later, bright and early Monday morning, Teagan gathered around the conference table with Secretary of State Shaw Asher, listening to President Sanders complain about missing weapons.

"I need answers," the president said, pacing in front of the oval office window while his Chief of Staff and the Vice President sat off to the side.

"As of right now, my channels have nothing, Sir," Teagan replied.

"Mr. President, it's not wise for you not to be involved," Secretary Linden counseled.

"It's already in the wind. The US will look like a laughing stock. Our soldiers will be killed, and our secrets will be leaked if the sale goes through!" President Sanders shouted.

"Then a different approach is needed," Linden said.

Teagan glanced at him. "A different approach?"

"Kill Yashan," Linden stated.

President Sanders waved him off. "On foreign soil? American spies will be executed in every country."

"If our weapons end up in terrorist hands, we've lost the battle no matter what," Linden snapped.

Teagan cleared her throat. "May I speak, Sir?"

President Sanders took a seat. "Go ahead."

"I made contact with Yashan and Mei Jing at the party. Do they trust me? No. But I would have a better chance of getting in at the auction if I showed up again."

"When does the auction take place?"

"In a few hours," Teagan replied.

"What if they recognize you? Better off going back to the house and killing him," Linden scoffed.

"Killing is the last resort. We know Morris Rogers met with Yashan and never showed up again."

"Oh, shit," Gregory muttered, staring at the TV.

All heads turned to the large screen on the side of the President's video call.

*"Breaking news. A dismembered body has been discovered. According to DNA evidence, it's the missing American, Morris Rogers,"* Sky News reported.

"Get the prime minister on the phone now!" President Sanders demanded from the Chief of Staff.

# Chapter Six

Wearing tactical pants, Teagan, Jude, and the rest of the team communicated silently that it was time to make their presence known. Jude had received a tip from a source about a meeting with the buyers Yashan had gathered to offload military weapons.

Teagan knew her cover would be blown once she entered, but not showing up would make things worse for President Sanders since his last year in office was quickly approaching. She'd worked for him for eight years, and a new leader would be in place soon that she would more than likely hate.

Motioning to her watch, they only had a few minutes to get in and out before it became a blood bath. Britain's Prime Minister had no idea what they were about to do, and President Sanders wanted to ensure plausible deniability if it blew up in their faces.

Teagan had no idea her vacation would end up like this as she approached the door in the alley late at night. If Christian saw her now, he'd have a fit and want her to come home. And she wouldn't fight him because she'd put her heart and soul into the Agency.

Gregory turned the knob slowly to open the door. Spider held his gun, ready to kill the first person who came at him. Teagan brought up the rear with Jude beside her. They took slow steps in the basement hallway of the abandoned building. A loud rumbling was heard, meaning Jude's contact was correct. Something was going down tonight, and the Agency would have first-hand knowledge. The stench of sewer water, rats, trash, and urine made Teagan want to gag as they pushed forward. The agency worked on different terms on foreign soil, and the rules only applied if they were caught.

Surveying the empty hall, Teagan thought it was strange how far they'd gotten without anyone noticing or being on lookout.

She raised her hand to halt everybody. "Made it down the hall for five minutes straight and no guard on duty," she whispered.

"You think it's a setup?" Jude inquired.

"I don't know."

"Splitting up might make it quicker and give us the advantage," Gregory suggested.

Teagan considered his plan and disregarded it. She had no control of the environment, and her goal was to get all her team safely back to America.

"We stick together," she answered, gesturing to continue down the hall.

Voices and laughter reached them, and she raised her hand again to silence the team. She waved for Gregory to come up front to determine the number of people they were dealing with. He removed his scope and passed Teagan the cell phone with the visual aid. It captured Yashan and Mei

Jing in discussion with six men surrounded by crates, which more than likely contained the stolen US weapons.

The team prepared their weapons as Gregory withdrew the scope lens and silently indicated the number of people with his fingers. Teagan gave a countdown from three, and they charged in with her guns raised, yelling for everyone to get on the ground.

"Put your hands up!"

"Police!" Mei Jing screamed, lifting her gun and shooting.

Jude took a bullet in the shoulder and dropped to the floor.

"On the ground!" Teagan shouted.

Some men ran, but Yashan picked up a gun from the crate, an automatic weapon, uncaring of who he hit. Diving for cover, Teagan fired shots at Yashan, who dragged one of his men in front of him for cover.

"Argghhhhhh!" The man fell, bleeding out.

Yashan took off down the hallway with Mei Jing close behind him.

Teagan jumped up and ran after them. "Stop!" Teagan screamed.

Mei whipped around and fired as they fled through the door into the alley.

Lungs heaving, Teagan reached the door, finding the alley empty. Tires squealed as a car disappeared around the corner. Cursing, Teagan lowered her weapon, wiping the sweat from her forehead as she retraced her steps to the basement. Dead bodies lay on the ground, surrounded by crates of guns.

Teagan picked up an ashtray with a cigar ashed out. "See if you can get fingerprints," she told Spider.

"The Prime Minister will be pissed." Jude huffed, clutching his injured shoulder.

"Can you keep this from him?" Teagan pleaded.

"I can keep it from the media but not from the prime minister." Jude winced in pain.

"Take him to the hospital."

Spider helped Jude stand, and Gregory wrapped a hand around his other arm to walk him to the car.

Spider grimaced. "They know your face now."

"I don't care."

"Our next step needs to be fast."

"He's ready to offload. The walls are closing in on him."

The basement was part of an old nightclub in London that had closed down a few years ago with the transition of Brexit. The guns they'd found were only the tip of the iceberg of Yashan's stash. Teagan ran her hand across the scratched-off serial numbers as the team checked the other crates.

Teagan closed her eyes. Her world was about to collide with the president and prime minister wanting answers.

* * *

*Same night.*

"What the fuck just happened?" Mei screamed, slamming the bedroom door in her suite. They hadn't planned for casualties. The authorities were now on high alert. Yashan dropped his holster on the couch and headed for the bar to fix a drink.

Mei narrowed her eyes, exasperated at being ignored.

She stomped over, snatched the drink from his hand, and tossed it across the room. "They found out!"

Yashan's eye twitched as he wrapped his hand around her neck and lifted her off the floor. "You stupid bitch." Mei clawed at his hands as he squeezed until her eyes rolled back in her head.

He released her suddenly, and she fell to the floor, coughing and sucking in air. "You almost killed me," she wheezed, crawling to the couch and grabbing his gun from the holster.

"I have no time for your antics, Mei," Yashan snapped.

She pointed the gun at his head. "I could kill you right now, and everyone would be grateful."

"And who will make you rich?" Yashan challenged. He pulled her toward him and pressed the gun into his chest. "President Zang would love to know that his number one advisor was making moves without him," he threatened through gritted teeth.

"Not if I kill you first," Mei hissed.

The door burst open, admitting Yashan's men.

Keeping his eyes locked on her, Yashan held up a hand to stall them. "We're fine. Right, Mei?"

Mei glared at him, desperate to end his life and find a different route to not being espoused. But she knew his men would kill her before she could pull the trigger.

"Yes. Everything is fine," she muttered.

"See? All good." Yashan waved his men back outside before moving back to the bar. He opened the bottle to pour a drink for Mei and himself. "I recognized the woman from the dinner with the prime minister and the president," he said, gulping his drink.

"She knows too much. You need to sell me the weapons, and I can offload them to China."

"Too risky."

Mei stood behind him. "For whom?"

"For you and me."

Mei tossed down the drink. She stalked back to the living room and plopped down on the couch. "I have a way for you to double your cut, and you're throwing it away."

Yashan slid out his phone, dialed a number, and brought it to his ear. "Do you have any information on the woman?"

"We followed them back to US Embassy," his man replied.

"Stay there."

"Yes, sir."

Mei hiked a brow as he ended the call.

"She's MI5 or CIA." Yashan placed his empty glass on the bar.

Mei stood, crossing her arms. "Then we need to ensure we kill her before it blows up for us."

"It's not just about the money."

Mei threw her hands in the air in frustration. "Then what do you want?"

Grinning, Yashan picked up the remote and turned on the TV to the latest news of an explosion in Sweden. "Worldwide destruction."

"The weapons will be linked to the USA."

He winked. "Exactly. The more I push the weapons around to cause an uproar that traces back to the US, the more the world will take notice. The Superpower that is America will no longer exist."

"How are you doing this?"

"I have someone who agrees with my alignment."

"Who?"

"Someone who owes me."

"Tell me."

"Not the right time."

"That's bullshit," Mei growled as Yashan walked to the door and opened it. "Forty million euros."

He turned to face her. "Forty million will get you one weapon."

"Fine, but I want to know who you're getting information from."

"That will cost you another twenty million."

Her eyes widened. "Ridiculous."

"My mission is worth more than your money."

"We'll see." She smirked as she walked around the couch and removed her shoes and pants.

"Are you flirting with me, Mei?" Yashan shut the door.

Tossing her shirt and pants aside, Mei pulled her shirt over her head, leaving it on the floor and sashaying down the hall to the bedroom. Yashan unbuckled his belt and loosened his vest.

Kicking the bedroom door open, Mei crawled on top of the bed in only her panties and bra with her back to Yashan.

"By the morning, we will be very familiar with each other, Yashan. I want to be on your team."

"Only if you can handle what I'm about to do, Mei Jing."

They grinned before slamming their mouths together in a sloppy kiss as they fell on the bed.

# Chapter Seven

A *week later*

Teagan sat, surrounded by soldiers, as President Sanders, Secretary of State Shaw, and Jude went back and forth on how to capture Yashan. President Sanders was pissed. The body reported by Sky News had been identified as Morris Rogers, and the stolen US weapons had caused the explosion in Sweden. Ambassador Asher pleaded with the Swedish government to give them time to discover what had happened before making any hasty decisions.

"Sending the agency to London was supposed to solve our problems, not start World War Three!" President Sanders argued.

The nervousness in the room heightened. No one wanted to speak while the president was on a tirade. Shaw fiddled with his phone. Ambassador Asher had the Swedish PM on the line, ready to talk, but having the president on edge would not help the situation.

Pictures of last night appeared on the screen—crates of guns and bullet holes littered the basement. Jude sent in a clean-up crew to ensure all trace of our involvement was wiped from the scene. America needed all its allies, and London was in the middle, with China laughing at us all.

Desperate to make her voice heard, Teagan angrily clicked the pen on the table. Not being on location with her men gnawed at her stomach.

"Teagan, what do you think?" President Sanders asked.

Coming out of her daze, Teagan placed the pen on the table and massaged her aching temples. "Deny it."

"What?"

Everybody in the room gasped in shock.

"Deny it," she repeated.

"Teagan, you're not looking at the whole picture," Shaw said.

"Sweden knows we're not responsible for what happened, Mr. President. Have the press secretary send a memo denying the US is behind the attack."

The president ran a hand over his face.

"I have to advise the president not to send any type of communication," Shaw urged.

"I have to agree with Asher," the president said. "We were already in a tight spot on the world stage."

Teagan responded, "We got close to him, Sir. We can catch him."

"Catch who?"

"Yashan."

"But you don't have him in custody right now, correct?"

"No, Mr. Secretary."

"Well, until we have him in custody, lowering our guard down will hurt our standing."

"Find him, Teagan, or you'll need to change course." President Sanders gestured to disconnect the call, and the screen went black.

Teagan stood and gathered everything to leave. Jude trailed her back to the office. Phones rang constantly, and reporters were outside the Embassy with cameras aimed at the doors, wanting to know how the US would respond.

"Looks like you could use a drink," Jude said, hovering in front of Teagan's desk.

Teagan turned on the computer to check her emails. "The guys went out to search for Mei."

"No leads yet?"

"No, and that worries me, Jude."

"They're the best."

Searching her desk, Teagan grabbed the remote to turn on the wall-mounted TV, waiting for video updates to be dispatched. "I have a feeling it was a trap."

"What do you mean?"

"It was too easy for us to leave that night. Yashan is known for not leaving any witnesses." She bit her lip as she tapped the remote idly on her hand. "Which means he might come after us."

"We'll be ready." Jude smiled and moved to place a reassuring hand on her shoulder.

A second later, her cell phone rang, and Teagan picked it up to a FaceTime call from Spider. "It's them."

"Patch it through." Jude faced the screen.

Teagan answered the Facetime call. "Spider put it through."

"Secure line?"

"In the office with Jude," Teagan answered.

Spider motioned behind him, and the call transferred to the TV screen.

"Arriving at the Sun Line Hotel for Mei Jing," Spider reported, climbing out of the black van.

The guys wore regular clothes over their protective gear to avoid drawing attention. They took the elevator, their expressions determined. Teagan's eyes never left the screen. The elevator doors peeled open. Daughtry's hand lingered near his gun on his hip as he knocked on the door. It swung open.

"Stand back," Daughtry commanded, removing his gun.

"Look. A trail of blood," Gregory announced.

Jude and Teagan glanced at each other.

"Daughtry, don't do anything stupid," Spider muttered, pulling his gun to cover him.

Broderick and Gregory stood guard at the front door. The camera panned to the bloodstains on the suite floor from a dead body.

"Remember not to touch anything," Teagan called through the speaker.

Treading slowly down the hall, Daughtry kicked the bedroom door open. The woman he was coming to arrest was dead on the bed with a bullet in her head.

"We have a problem," Daughtry announced.

"Tell me," Teagan demanded.

Daughtry shook his head, entering the room to scope the closet and bathroom. Spider came up behind, checking for clues.

"Mei is dead," Daughtry announced.

"Shit," Teagan cursed.

"No evidence of a break-in. More than likely, it was Yashan," Spider explained, holding up a cell phone from the nightstand.

"Gregory, make sure you download everything from her phone," Teagan reminded him.

Daughtry lifted her briefcase from the closet. "Nothing here but clothes and files on her work with the Chinese president."

"We can make copies for President Sanders before returning them to China. An opportunity like this doesn't come often," Teagan said.

Jude pressed a finger to mute the call. "Think about what you're about to do, Teagan."

"What is it you think I'm doing wrong?"

"China and US relations aren't the best. It's only a matter of time before it gets to President Zang. Something is off about the killing."

"Off how?"

"Yashan could be setting you up." Jude waved his hand at the screen.

"We have everything on camera."

Jude removed his hand from the mute button and rubbed his forehead. "Let me get my guys there first."

"But—"

"Believe me, it can work. We need to establish a transfer of intelligence between the Agency and the Chinese government once they're notified of Mei Jing's death," Jude said, dialing his cell phone.

"Say we do it your way, and President Zang still wants our heads for being at the location."

Jude grabbed a pen and paper. "There's no reason for him to make it a bigger situation unless Mei Jing was doing something she shouldn't have."

Teagan waited for Jude to finish calling for backup. Spider, Daughtry, and the rest of the team continued searching the room and dusting for prints.

* * *

Kicking off her shoes and peeling off her jacket, Teagan strolled to the telephone and snatched the hotel menu off the table to order room service. She was exhausted from the long day of reading over every document Mei had in her possession. Gregory downloaded most of her cell phone data and transcribed the behind-the-scenes deals and plans without President Zang's backing.

"Room service," the hotel concierge answered.

"Hi, this is Director Stone in suite forty-three."

"Yes, Mrs. Stone."

"I'd love to get the same thing I ordered last night. Soup and a salad with a glass of wine."

"Yes, ma'am. We'll be right up."

"Thank you." Teagan hung up and tucked her feet under her on the couch. She pressed the TV remote to find something to watch while calling her family back home.

"Hey, babe," Christian answered.

"Hi. Sorry to ring you at work." It was eight pm in London and one pm in New York.

"Just finished up a meeting. I have time to talk to my beautiful wife," Christian teased.

"Not so beautiful at the moment."

"You sound tired. Long day?"

Teagan nodded even though he couldn't see her. "Yes, a lot of paperwork."

"Have you eaten?"

"Ordered room service. It should arrive in the next few minutes."

"Good. Any idea when you'll be heading home?"

"Probably in the next few days if we can't come up with any answers."

"I can't say I'm unhappy about you coming home."

A knock on the door interrupted her before she could reply. Checking the peephole, she saw the room service attendant and opened the door.

"Director Stone, we have soup and salad." The attendant removed the lid covering the food and stood aside for her to check out.

"Babe, give me one second," Teagan said to Christian, pressing the mute button and reaching into her purse for a tip.

"Thank you," the attendant said.

"Of course," Teagan answered, shutting the door. She picked up the food tray, placed it on the table, and unmuted the call. "How are the kids?" She dipped the spoon into the tomato soup and started to eat.

"Tatum and Cole are ready for you to come home."

Teagan uncorked the wine, poured it into the glass, and took several large gulps. "Tell Tatum to stay out of my makeup and make sure Cole is taking a bath."

"Your son is hardheaded."

"Takes after his father." Teagan hiccupped as the wine took its desired effect.

"Call me tomorrow, my love."

"I love you, Christian."

"Love you more, Tee."

Feeling good, Teagan relaxed. She stared at the ceiling, feeling like her life was finally going in the direction she'd hoped.

# Chapter Eight

The next morning, Teagan groggily removed her eye mask over her head to a pounding on the door on her door. Grunting, she threw off the covers and pulled on her robe, her head pounding as she staggered to the door.

"Do you know what time it is?" she barked as she opened the door to Daughtry and Spider.

"We have something you have to see?" Daughtry said, ignoring her bad mood.

"What is it?" Teagan snatched the recording device from his hand while Spider placed a takeout coffee in her other hand.

Sitting on the couch, she sipped her coffee and waited for one of them to explain why they'd woken her, especially if it wasn't a life-or-death situation.

"We uncovered information on Mei's phone which proved that she was working with Yashan," Spider explained.

Teagan's shoulders slumped. "That was long established."

"Yashan had contingency plans if Mei tried to screw him over." Spider sat beside her and opened his laptop.

"Mei used me as a target to obtain information." Daughtry took the chair and propped his elbows on his knees, waiting for the video to start.

"Go on." Teagan took another sip of coffee.

"It all comes down to Morris Rogers." Spider pointed at the screen, where Morris was talking to someone in an office.

"Who is Morris talking to?"

"General Raymond Hives. Morris Rogers' uncle." Spider turned the volume up on the computer.

*"Remember why you have the power to make things right, Morris."*

*"I promise to ensure we're good on our end."*

*"That's great, but Yashan is a dangerous man, and if he smells you trying to back out, it could fall apart."*

*Morris's brows lowered in confusion. "You've made him understand, right? Our goal is the money."*

*General Hives patted him on the cheek, grabbed the cigar sitting in the ashtray, and took a puff.*

*"I gave my life to this flag. Bullets flying over my head every day. Battle scars ensuring people's freedom."*

*"I know." Morris shifted uneasily.*

*The General moved to the window in his office at the Navy base. "Do you know how sad it is that we have to send messages to make people understand what can happen if you don't follow the rules?"*

*"If Yashan cheats us out of the money, we'll need a backup plan."*

*"He won't."*

*"How do you know?"*

*"Yashan is a man of his word."*

*"All right. I need to hurry and catch my flight before it's too late."* Morris hugged his uncle and left his office.

*Blowing out more smoke, General Hives smiled. The phone rang, and he placed the call on speaker.*

*"Do we have a deal?" Yashan asked.*

*General Hives put out his cigar. "The money is secondary to what we talked about."*

*"Always, my friend."*

*"Good. Morris has the information, and once you take care of him, I want visual confirmation on where the weapons are going," General Hives said.*

*"Sweden, China, and London are the first stops," Yashan replied.*

*"Fantastic. Sanders won't suspect a thing."*

*"And Morris?"*

*The general paused. "What about him?"*

*"He can't walk away."*

*"Good. He needs to learn not to play in a man's world."*

*The line went dead.*

*A long-established decorated officer, General Hives was the best of the best in the military, and the team would always wonder what made him go off the deep end.*

Turning off the screen, Spider and Daughtry waited for Teagan's response. "How did you get the footage?"

"Gregory got a red flag alert while tracing Morris's whereabouts. He had a camera hidden in his uncle's office for exactly this situation."

Teagan rewatched the video. "He never trusted him."

"Only reason I can see." Spider knuckles beat on the table.

Daughtry got up and reached for the bottle of water off the counter, taking a drink. "I figure Mei got the footage from my phone. I didn't know it was there until Gregory got the alert."

Teagan sighed. "All this time, we had the smoking gun."

Spider nodded. "We were too busy chasing Yashan when we should've done a deeper dive into Morris's background."

"Damn." Teagan slumped on the couch.

"So what's next?" Daughtry asked.

"I need to shower and get myself together."

"President needs to know," Daughtry suggested.

Teagan rose from the couch. "He's probably in a meeting."

"Yashan is planning on going to China, then London. We have the evidence." Spider gestured at the screen.

"Get Jude on the line and call a meeting with President Zang."

Daughtry and Spider looked at Teagan in surprise.

"What?" Teagan folded her arms over her chest.

"Yashan is probably on his way out of the country," Spider pointed out.

"We need to get all parties on the same page and work together. If we tip anyone off, Yashan will strike."

Picking up his phone, Spider started making calls.

"Daughtry, get the team ready." Teagan headed to the bedroom to shower and get dressed for the day.

* * *

Out in the field, Yashan talked with his men as they loaded up dump trucks with weapons hidden in crates. It was almost midnight, and taking care of Mei and finalizing his deal with General Hines was the last item on his agenda before he flew home. Waving his hands for the drivers to head out, he puffed on the cigar, uncaring of the political ramifications of his actions.

A smirk pulled at his mouth as he remembered putting a bullet in Mei's head when he found the recording she'd stolen from his phone. He jumped into his car, feeling pleasure at the scandal Britain and the world would have to deal with. Answering his phone, Yashan stayed alert as his driver left the warehouse.

"How are we looking?" General Hines didn't bother with small talk.

"On time."

"You made a big mess today," General Hines chastised.

Yashan shrugged. "Had to be done."

Driving through the streets at night, he'd made sure to have the police on the payroll so they would look the other way.

"Make sure we have no complications," General Hines ordered.

"You did your part. I have it from here."

"President Zang is not happy. I applaud you for making a big move." General Hines chuckled.

"A war between countries will make us a lot of money," Yashan agreed.

The light turned red, and Yashan's driver waited, tapping his hand on the steering wheel. As the truck ahead pulled through the lights, motorcycles appeared from nowhere, and gunfire erupted.

"Go! Go!" Yashan shouted, pissed that someone was trying to take him out. Swerving to the right, his driver took a side road to catch up to the dump truck. Two motorcyclists wearing black sped up, sending warning shots.

"What the hell is going on?" General Hines barked.

"Are you setting me up?" Yashan demanded, dropping the phone on the seat. He grabbed his gun, opened the limo sunroof, and stood to return fire at the motorcycles.

"Yashan! Yashan!" General Hines yelled, but Yashan ignored him.

The driver wove in and out of traffic as the motorcycles tried to cut him off. Each rider wore a black mask. Yashan figured it was the Americans coming after him. Hearing his phone ringing, he dropped back down to answer.

"Give yourself up and negotiate."

"Who is this?" Yashan hissed at the authoritative female voice.

Teagan sat in the back of the black van trailing Yashan's vehicle. Daughtry, Spider, and Broderick rode on motorcycles with other MI5 agents. All the roads were locked down as Yashan sent his men on a suicide mission.

"Someone who knows the outcome if you don't stop right now."

Grimacing, Yashan put the phone on mute and closed the sunroof. "Take me to the railway station."

"We're too far from the checkpoint," his driver said.

Yashan pressed the gun to his head. "Do as I say!"

He nodded, making a swift turn toward Eurostar Station.

"You can't run, Yashan," Teagan taunted.

"Who are you?"

Teagan waited a few seconds before answering. "Finally, we get to introduce ourselves." She watched multiple monitors capture all five trucks going to different areas.

Yashan chortled. "Please. I'd like to know the person I'm about to kill."

"American spy for the US president, Agent Stone."

"Ah, an American spy. Mei Jing was right about you."

"She was."

"Well, American spy Agent Stone, you'll have to excuse me for not staying on the phone longer."

"Your plan won't work."

"Let me be the judge of that." Yashan ended the call and threw his phone out the window.

His driver hit a motorcycle, causing traffic to back up and giving them an opening to escape. Minutes later, they arrived at the train station.

Yashan hopped out and looked around the area for any police. "Let's go!" he commanded, sprinting toward the train.

# Chapter Nine

Spider helped Broderick from the ground after being hit by Yashan's vehicle. The van pulled up next to them, and they jumped aboard. Broderick sat down to check out his wounds.

"We lost him," Spider announced, removing his mask.

"He knows there are only two ways out of here." Teagan stared at the monitors, scanning the routes Yashan could have taken.

"Where's Daughtry?" Spider asked.

"Still out there." Teagan twisted the knob on the radio to get a signal.

"There he is." Gregory pointed at the screen. Each team member was equipped with a surveillance device. Daughtry jumped off his bike and ran onto the train as the doors closed.

"Daughtry, don't go in there alone," Teagan warned too late.

"Got him!" Gregory shouted, scanning faces as people boarded the train.

"Faster!" Teagan urged their driver.

They drove through a red light, narrowly avoiding a collision. It was Friday night, and the traffic was impeding them.

"Jude, we need the train stopped." Teagan looked over her shoulder at him.

"It's out of my hands, Teagan." Broderick winced at the pain in his shoulder.

Gregory and Teagan watched as Daughtry had security stop the train before it left the station.

Police sirens reached them from behind the van. Great. Just what they needed while they were in a foreign country chasing a terrorist.

"Don't stop," Teagan ordered. "Our guys need us." She pointed at Yashan, pushing through the crowd on the train. The van reached the station, and Teagan pulled out her gun.

Jude placed his hand on her shoulder. "Go, I can handle the police."

"Are you sure?"

"My ass is on the line, but who cares?" Jude smirked.

Teagan, Spider, and Gregory ran into the station, ignoring the police as they shouted at them not to move. They caught up with Daughtry as he was being arrested.

"Watch it!" Teagan yelled, shoving people out of the way.

"Back up, or you'll be arrested," the police officer holding Daughtry in handcuffs shouted at Teagan.

"Spider, come with me. Gregory, you deal with him," Teagan huffed.

They took off through the crowd. Spider spotted Yashan with his driver. Teagan saw him too, and they pushed through the passengers.

Teagan motioned at Spider as she raised her gun. "Be careful. We have too many people here."

Spider nodded. "I'll take the left."

The driver glared at Teagan. "His friend is not happy to see us."

"Maybe we should make an entrance."

"No one can get hurt," Teagan announced.

Yashan grinned, raised his gun, and fired. Passengers screamed and dispersed in all directions as the train pulled out of the station.

"My God. He has a gun!" a lady screamed, backing away.

Yashan snatched a young woman and pointed the gun at her head. His driver snagged a kid and aimed the gun at his chest, ready to pull the trigger. The train wheels squealed as someone hit the emergency stop.

"Agent Stone, we meet under such terrible situations." Yashan loved playing games.

"Let them go, Yashan," Teagan demanded, glancing around at the confused and scared faces.

"Put your gun down," Yashan instructed, wrapping his hand around the neck of his hostage.

"Please, let me go," the woman cried.

Yashan shushed her and kissed her cheek.

"You won't leave here alive, Yashan," Teagan called.

Police surrounded the train. Teagan and Spider made eye contact, knowing that what happened next could end up with everyone dead.

"No matter what you do, I win," Yashan taunted, pulling a radio from his pocket and sending word to his men to set off the explosions.

"Yashan!" Spider shouted, distracting him as Teagan inched toward him.

"Move one more step, and she dies," Yashan growled.

"Please!" the girl pleaded.

"What's your name?" Teagan asked gently.

"Anna."

"Anna, I'm so sorry," Teagan said right before she shot Anna in the shoulder. The woman screamed and slumped to the ground. Without hesitating, Spider and Teagan shot Yashan multiple times. The driver yelled and went to kill the boy, but the police burst in behind him and wrestled him to the ground.

Spider ran to Anna. Teagan checked Yashan's pulse. He was dead, his blood pooling around him. More police arrived, along with paramedics who moved to help Anna.

"News won't like what happened tonight," Spider said.

Wiping the sweat off her brow. "Neither do I."

* * *

Teagan knocked on the hospital room door, nodding at the policeman on duty outside.

"Come in."

Covered in a hospital gown, Anna lay in bed recovering from her gunshot wound. The news was on the TV, replaying the events at the train station the night before.

"How are you feeling?" Teagan asked.

"Sore," Anna replied with a grimace.

"I'm so sorry. I brought you some food and flowers."

"It's not your fault."

"My job is complicated, but I never want anyone in harm's way."

"At first, I was shocked, and my parents are still upset, but I know you did what needed to be done."

"The press thinks I'm crazy." Teagan pointed at the TV.

"Yeah, they'll probably revoke your passport." Anna laughed.

"Believe me, it'll be a while before I return to London."

"Are you flying home?" Anna inquired.

"Yes. We've retrieved all of the weapons Yashan stole."

"Never in my life did I imagine myself involved in something like last night."

Teagan understood how she felt, remembering her first mission. Now, she was used to the wild ride.

"Thank you for saving me." Anna picked over the hospital food on her tray.

Teagan smiled and patted her leg before leaving the room. She told the policeman to keep an eye on Anna in case Yashan's allies tried to finish her off. Jumping in the car, she headed to the airport to fly home. A few things needed to be wrapped up before she could close the case.

The next day, Teagan and Spider went to visit General Hines. As they approached his office door, a gunshot rang out.

Teagan tried the door handle, but it was locked. "Bust it open."

Teagan drew her gun and stood back while Spider kicked the door open. General Hines was slumped over his desk with blood oozing from a bullet wound in his head.

"Looks like he took the easy way out." Spider gestured to the gun in his hand.

The TV was on, reporting that Yashan and General Hines knew each other and had been instrumental in Morris's death. The general had gone from a decorated soldier to a disgrace, all because of greed.

"Pack everything up." Teagan flipped through files in General Hines's office.

"Teagan, he left a note." Spider pointed at the envelope on the desk.

"Give it to the president," Teagan said. "I'm going home to be with my family."

# Chapter Ten

<br>

A Month Later

Teagan stood in front of the washing machine, reading Cole's report card and eating an apple.

The case against General Hines and Yashan was still under review, but Teagan's involvement with the shooting of Anna had been closed without any charges. Anna didn't file a complaint, and the prime minister and President Sanders quietly made her an offer never to talk about what happened that night.

Folding the second load of towels, Teagan walked out of the basement and went into the living room, where the kids were watching TV.

"Did you three eat your breakfast?" Teagan inquired.

"Yes, Mom!" All three answered at the same time.

Teagan sat on the loveseat, holding the basket of towels to separate for each bathroom.

"Mom, can we go outside and play?" Tatum scooted up on the couch, facing her mom. "Sure, Tatum, but stay out front so I can see."

"I will!" Tatum said excitedly, running outside.

"Cole, great job at school. Your teacher said you're the most improved student."

"Does that mean I can have ice cream?" Cole begged.

Teagan laughed at his puppy dog eyes. "Sure, but only two scoops. I have lunch almost ready."

"Mom, are you coming to my away game tomorrow?" CJ asked.

Teagan didn't recall anything on the family calendar. "Where is it again?"

"DC," CJ replied, his attention on his video game.

"Oh, right. Your dad forgot to tell me. What time is the game?"

"Three."

"Are you packed?" Teagan bent to kiss his forehead.

"Yes, ma'am."

"Cool. Let me go find your father."

Heading to his office, Teagan knocked softly, hearing him talking on the phone. Entering quietly, she moved to sit on the edge of his desk.

"Robert, Teagan just walked in. Let me call you back," Christian said, ending the call. Smiling at his wife, he pulled her onto his lap, and she laughed at his playfulness.

"That smile says I need to just say yes," Christian jested.

"I forgot about CJ's game in DC."

"What do you have to do?"

"Lunch and catch up with the President."

"How long is it going to take?"

"Hopefully not too long, but CJ's game is at three, and the meeting is at one."

"Can you see about pushing it up earlier?"

Teagan cocked her head. "You want me to tell the President to push his schedule up?"

"Yes, and you have no choice."

"How so?"

"Last game of the season, and he wants you there."

"Damn."

"Damn, indeed. What's for lunch?"

"Bangers and mash," Teagan teased.

Christian laughed. "You're kidding, right?"

"Nope. I didn't get to enjoy London as a family because of work."

"You're turning into a British aristocrat," Christian complained. He patted her thigh to stand up and followed her out of his office. Holding hands, they entered the living room to see CJ with his head still in his game and Cole eating ice cream next to him.

Teagan pulled out plates and silverware to set the table. "Stop complaining and get the kids ready for lunch."

Cole and CJ came to sit at the table, and Tatum ran through the open back door to the sink to wash her hands.

"Boys, wash your hands." Teagan put a pitcher of water on the table.

Christian sat at the head of the table, fixing plates while Teagan poured everyone a glass of water.

"Mom, when's the next vacation?" Tatum kicked her legs back and forth in her chair.

"I don't know. Where do you want to go?" Teagan placed the napkin in her lap.

"Maybe Dubai."

"Why Dubai, Tatum?" Christian asked.

Tatum shrugged. "My friends say it's pretty."

"What friends?"

"Friends in school, Daddy."

"Little girl, what friends do you have whose parents can afford to go to Dubai?" Christian joked.

Everybody laughed. "Missy and Korrie's family went to Dubai for their birthday." Tatum cut into her food.

"When you're a little older, baby." Teagan helped Tatum to wipe her mouth.

"Mom, you're on TV with the president." Cole pointed at the TV in the living room.

All eyes turned to see President Sanders in front of the podium and Teagan with her team standing in the back.

"I see." Teagan got out of the chair, went into the living room, and turned off the TV to enjoy time with her family.

* * *

The family and the team flew to DC the next day. Teagan was exhausted after getting up early to ensure the kids were ready before packing her things to meet with the President. The kids slept most of the way, and she and Christian talked throughout.

Leaving the plane, Teagan got in a private Escalade while Jason stayed behind with Spider. She specifically wanted Daughtry and Gregory with her for the meeting with President Sanders.

Before heading to the White House, they dropped Christian and the kids at the hotel with their luggage. All eyes were on them as police escorts took them through the traffic.

"Still not talking to me?" Daughtry's eyes met hers.

Teagan had already decided she would take the blame

for any fallout from Daughtry's slip-up. "Never not talking to you, Daughtry. But you need to be more careful."

The security gate opened for them as they arrived at the White House. Teagan, Daughtry, and Gregory climbed out of the car and shook hands with the assistant chief of staff.

He gestured down the hall. "President Sanders is waiting for you in the oval office."

Secret Service opened the door, allowing entry as the president sat with Chief of Staff Linden and Secretary of State Shaw.

"Agent Stone. I see only two of your team members." President Sanders shook hands with each of them.

"Mr. President, you remember Daughtry and Gregory."

"Take a seat, please," President Sanders instructed.

"Agent Stone, we're not sure if you've watched the news," the chief of staff said.

"No, I haven't," Teagan answered.

"Even though you thwarted Vasiliev's mission, a few things came to light," President Sanders continued.

Daughtry and Teagan knew he was talking about Mei Jing and Daughtry's stolen phone.

"Should the contents have gotten out, we'd be having a different conversation," Shaw pointed out.

"Daughtry knows he messed up. It won't happen again," Teagan stated.

President Sanders frowned. "He still put himself in a compromising position. He knows how crucial his job is and how easy it is to be compromised."

"Your services are terminated, Daughtry," Linden announced.

"Sir—"

Teagan raised her hand to interrupt Daughtry. "Secretary Shaw, I don't believe Daughtry's actions warrant termination. He was pivotal in bringing down Yashan."

"Then we have a difference of opinion because the President agrees with me," Linden insisted.

Teagan felt the rug being pulled from under her. She fixed her gaze on Linden. "Director Stone is my job title, correct?"

"What does that have to do with anything?" he snipped.

"It means that I make the decisions inside the firm."

"I think you misunderstand, Director Stone," Shaw said through clenched teeth.

Teagan looked between Linden, Shaw, and the president. "If Daughtry is fired, you can expect my resignation on your desk tomorrow morning."

President Sanders' mouth thinned, and he shook his head.

"I refuse to allow you to make Daughtry a scapegoat," Teagan said firmly.

Daughtry sighed. "Teagan, it's all right."

"No. I want it understood that I decide how I run the firm, or I'll step down."

"No need. You're fired," Secretary Linden snapped,

"As you wish." Teagan raised her chin and stood to leave the room.

"You don't need to quit because of me, Teagan. I can take the suspension," Daughtry urged.

"I won't stay knowing I have no say in how I run my office," Teagan insisted.

A muscle ticked in President Sanders' jaw. "Fine. Daughtry has a one-week suspension."

"On full pay," Teagan bargained.

The president sighed. "Fine," he repeated.

Teagan nodded. "I'll remain as director for now, but you need to find a replacement for me soon."

President Sanders smiled. "As if anyone could replace you."

* * *

"Were you really going to quit?" Daughtry asked once they were in the car.

"I was."

Teagan pulled out her phone and updated Spider as they made their way to the game to watch CJ.

"We're here, Director Stone," Jason notified her several minutes later.

"Thanks, Jason."

Teagan pushed all thoughts of business from her mind and enjoyed being a mom and wife for the next few hours.

# Chapter Eleven

**M**onths later.

Teagan and Christian watched from home as President Sanders shook hands with the President of China. A deal had been brokered between the two countries to combat illegal imports.

The boys were out playing, and Tatum was curled up next to Teagan on the couch, drinking hot chocolate. The temperature had dropped, bringing snow, and the schools were closed.

"I have to fly to DC in a week," Teagan murmured. "I'm submitting my resignation."

Christian looked at her in shock. "Seriously?"

Teagan smiled. "It's time."

Christian rubbed her neck. "I thought President Sanders refused to let you go."

"He won't have a choice with the upcoming debates and the election cycle."

"Too busy to keep an eye on his favorite spy?" Christian teased.

Teagan smiled. "I feel good about my decision."

Christian kissed her. "You know I'll support whatever you decide."

"Thank you."

"How is Daughtry handling riding the desk?"

"He was pissed at first, but he understood why when I told him Linden was still trying to push his own agenda."

"Shaw running for President is surprising."

"Not to me."

"Why?"

"President Sanders was letting him take the lead more and more," Teagan observed.

Christian tapped her temple. "That spy brain works overtime."

She grinned. "It never stops."

He kissed her again. "Ready to go?"

"Yep. You're driving, right?"

"For sure. Family outing to the circus."

Laughing, Teagan stood and tugged Christian up from the couch.

"Circus time!" Tatum danced around the room.

Teagan high-fived her daughter and pulled her into a hug.

"From fighting the bad guys to the circus," Christian joked.

Teagan called the boys, and they piled into the car while Jason followed in another vehicle with security. For once, it felt like a regular family outing, and Christian loved seeing the smiles on the kids' faces. He turned up the radio, and the kids danced in their seats to the latest music from artists on TikTok.

Teagan hated how fast the kids were growing up and

wanted to enjoy these moments forever. She couldn't wait to be a stay-at-home mom.

Christian linked her hand with his, raising it to his mouth and kissing her knuckles.

An hour later, Christian pulled up in the circus parking lot.

"You think Jason and the guys will like the circus," Christian asked, seeing them huddled up together, whispering.

"Probably not." Teagan laughed.

They approached the booth and showed their tickets, but a hand landed on Teagan's shoulder as they headed inside.

"Director Stone," Jason said.

Teagan and Christian glanced at each other.

"Is it an emergency, Jason?" Teagan asked, keeping her eyes on Christian.

"Ma'am, I have the president's secretary on the phone."

Teagan sighed. "Take the kids inside. I'll meet up with you."

"Teagan, come on. It's the circus." Christian grumbled.

"Mom, are you coming with us?" Tatum asked.

Teagan took the phone from Jason. "I'll be there in a second, honey."

Teagan stepped out of the line as Christian escorted the kids inside. "Hello."

"Director Stone?"

"Yes."

"We have you scheduled to fly out tomorrow morning to meet with Secretary Shaw," the president's secretary explained.

"Tomorrow?" Teagan asked sharply.

"Yes. There's an emergency that can't wait."

"We're scheduled for next week."

"Plans have changed."

"What's wrong?"

"I can't discuss it over the line."

Teagan's pulse quickened. "Tell me now, or I won't be on that plane."

"President Sanders can explain better."

"Teagan." The president joined the call.

"Sir, I'm with my family."

"I couldn't wait until next week."

"Is something wrong?"

"My family is going to be destroyed."

Teagan's head reared back at his statement. "I can only help if you tell me what's wrong."

"I'm retiring before the election."

*"What?"*

"Come to DC, and I'll explain. Please."

"I can't—"

"Look at this! It's the president!" a woman shouted, holding up a cell phone as people gathered around her.

Approaching the woman, Teagan peered over her shoulder to see a video of President Sanders and a woman in a compromising position.

"Get the plane ready," Teagan told the president.

Sending her husband a text, she had Jason drive her to the airport while she watched breaking news of President Sanders' fall from grace.

The coverage switched to President Sanders giving a speech with his family beside him.

*"I would like to apologize to my family and the American people. What I did was a mistake, and I take respon-*

*sibility.”*

* * *

“We’re months away from twenty-four debates.” Teagan clasped her hands on her lap.

“Which is why President Sanders wants to ensure the Agency stays open,” Linden replied.

Teagan sat up straight. “I didn’t know it was in jeopardy of closing.”

The news of the firm possibly closing shocked her to silence. Glancing between both gentlemen, she waited for answers and pondered if it could hurt the team. Years of her life and the team poured into the firm.

President Sanders took an envelope from Linden and handed it to Teagan.

“What am I looking at?” she asked.

“A few years ago, I stepped out on my wife when I was a Senator.” President Sanders ran a hand through his hair.

Teagan was quiet as she sifted through the photos in the envelope. They showed the same woman in the video with the president. She was a reporter for GNS, and speculation was rife that President Sanders had been feeding her information throughout his tenure.

“The news reporter,” Teagan muttered.

“You can’t retire, Teagan,” President Sanders pleaded.

Teagan looked at the president. “What a way to end a career.”

“I’ll take the hit and leave with what’s left of my dignity. I need you to stay for the new administration. I want the firm intact after I’m gone,” President Sanders muttered.

"You'll answer to Secretary Shaw until a new president is elected," Linden stated. "Is that a problem?"

"Yes."

"No one can see what's ahead of us, but we need to show a united front now China and the US are on friendly terms again. We'll look weak if we close the firm," the president reasoned.

Teagan shook her head. "My life is not the firm."

"I told you we should find someone else," Linden grumbled.

"Enough!" the president snapped. He fixed his gaze on Teagan. "One last time. Please."

Teagan paused, seeing the sorrow in his eyes. "One last time?"

President Sanders grinned. "For the agency."

Teagan nodded. "Director Stone, at your service, Sir."

* * *

I hope you've enjoyed Teagan's story so far. Please also check out "**Mirror of Lust Book 2**" https://book s2read.com/u/mVRpz2 with a host of characters intertwined.

Also, if you love Mystery and Suspense, check out **Mirror of Lies Book 1** https://books2read.com/u/ mgjEPx"

Another thriller crime fiction, "**Ruined** https://book s2read.com/u/bzVGAj"

Check out the free short here, *"The Firm"* https://payhip.com/b/py7S

Grab Boxset "**Agent Red 1-3**" here https://payhip.com/b/1KcxY

Grab Boxset "**Agent Red 4-6**" here https://book s2read.com/u/m2qBPk

# Sneak Peek: Mirror of Danger
## Book 3

Jessica returned to work after the kidnapping and the death of her best friends. Now it was time to go back full time as a journalist and put her mind on the job. It only made sense when a story dropped in her lap to continue finding out what the police had missed. The biggest story across the news stations caused her to not only be the face in the media, but someone had other plans that derailed her into danger.

Can Jessica put her life back on track once again?

# What's Next?

Want to know what happens next? Follow me at the links below to catch the next release.

Thank you so much for reading, and if you enjoyed the crazy ride and decide to leave a review, we truly appreciate the support. Reviews are the lifeblood of the publishing world. They're read, appreciated, and needed. Please consider taking the time to leave a few words on Goodreads or BookBub.

Sign up for updates and sneak peeks at the sites below:

www.authoravasking.com
www.bookbub.com/avasking
www.goodreads.com/author/avasking
www.Twitter.com/authoravaking
www.Instagram.com/authoravasking
www.Facebook.com/authoravasking
www.304publishing.tumblr.com

# Teagan Stone Reading Order of Series

1.Agent Red—Fatal Memory Book 1
https://books2read.com/u/4j2PYX
2.Agent Red—Fatal Target Book 2
https://books2read.com/u/bWP8Jq
3.Agent Red—Fatal Crime Book 3
https://books2read.com/u/mZadZJ
4.Agent Red—Fatal Justice Book 4
https://books2read.com/u/mqo7wd
5.Agent Red—Fatal Enemy Book 5
https://books2read.com/u/bxeo1q
6. Agent Red—Fatal Death Book 6
https://books2read.com/u/mqwlRv
7. Agent Red—Fatal Revenge Book 7
https://books2read.com/u/3JnKyA
8. Agent Red—Fatal Pursuit Book 8
https://books2read.com/u/bOPowo
9. Agent Red—Fatal Attack Book 9
10. Agent Red—Fatal Mission Book 10

# Reading Order of Mirror Series

Mirror of Lies Book 1
https://books2read.com/u/mgjEPx
Mirror of Lust Book 2
https://books2read.com/u/mVRpz2
Mirror of Danger Book 3
Mirror of Murder Book 4

# Acknowledgments

I want to thank my team, who helps me behind the scenes, from my editors to my test readers and graphic designers, and the list goes on. I truly appreciate each of you for keeping me on my toes.

# About the Author

Ava S. King is the debut author of thriller, mystery, suspense, and psychological crime novels.

If you want to know when the next book will come out, please visit the Author Ava S.King website at http://www.authoravasking.com, where you can sign up to receive an email for her next release.

# About 304 Publishing Company

We showcase authors writing romance, women's fiction, horror, erotica, crime fiction, fantasy, paranormal, sifi, thrillers, suspense novels, poetry collections, and beauty & style books.

Join our mailing list to stay updated with new releases and blog posts.

www.ingramcontent.com/pod-product-compliance
Lightning Source LLC
Chambersburg PA
CBHW011225190726
48287CB00008B/2756